14.95

EVANSTON PUBLIC LIBRARY

3 1192 00961 5731

x949.7024 Isaac.J

Isaac, John.

Bosnia : civil war in
Europe /

D1611261

DATE DUE	
DEC 9 - 1998	
OCT 6 - 2003	
6/16/12	

DEMCO, INC. 38-2931

MAY 0 6 1997

CHILDREN IN CRISIS

BOSNIA

Civil War in Europe

Photos by John Isaac
Text by
Keith Greenberg

A B L A C K B I R C H P R E S S B O O K

W O O D B R I D G E , C O N N E C T I C U T

EVANSTON PUBLIC LIBRARY
CHILDREN'S DEPARTMENT
1703 ORRINGTON AVENUE
EVANSTON, ILLINOIS 60201

Published by Blackbirch Press, Inc.
260 Amity Road
Woodbridge, CT 06525
©1997 Blackbirch Press, Inc.

First Edition

All rights reserved. No part of this book may be reproduced in any form with-out permission in writing from Blackbirch Press, Inc., except by a reviewer.

Printed in the United States of America

10 9 8 7 6 5 4 3 2

Photo credits on page 32

Library of Congress Cataloging-in-Publication Data
Isaac, John.
    Bosnia: civil war in Europe/photos by John Isaac; text by Keith Green-berg.—1st ed.
        p.   cm. — (Children in crisis)
    Summary: A United Nations photographer in Bosnia describes the conflict there, the bitterness among the ethnic/religious groups, and the plights of the victims, particularly children.
        ISBN 1-56711-186-6 (lib. bdg. : alk. paper)
        1. Yugoslav War, 1991—Bosnia and Herzegovina—Juvenile lit-erature. 2. Bosnia and Herzegovina—Ethnic relations—Juvenile literature. 3. Yugoslav War, 1991—Children—Juvenile literature.
    [1. Yugoslav War, 1991—Bosnia and Herzegovina. 2. Bosnia and Herzegovina—Ethnic relations.] I. Greenberg, Keith Elliot.
      II. Title. III. Series.
      DR1313.3.I78   1997   96-4239
        949.702'4—dc20   CIP
                                             AC

Opposite: Eleven-year-old Adisa heads back to her room in a makeshift Muslim camp in Resnik, Croatia. When this photo was taken, she had not seen her father for more than five months.

Austria

Hungary

SLOVENIA

Romania

• Zagreb

Vojvodina

CROATIA

Belgrade

BOSNIA–
HERZEGOVINA

SERBIA

YUGOSLAVIA

Sarajevo •

Adriatic Sea

MONTENEGRO

Bulgaria

Italy

Kosovo

Albania

MACEDONIA

Greece

Europe

*Atlantic
Ocean*

Bosnia

☐ Former Yugoslavia

• Capital city

A LOOK AT BOSNIA

osnia—also known as Bosnia and Herzegovina—is located in what was once the nation of Yugoslavia, in the Balkans region of southeastern Europe. From 1918 to 1991, Bosnia was one of six Yugoslavian republics, along with Croatia, Macedonia, Montenegro, Serbia, and Slovenia. In March 1992, Bosnia declared its independence. Now, it is bordered on the north and west by Croatia, and on its east and south by the countries of Serbia and Montenegro.

Bosnia is shaped like a triangle and is about one half the size of Kentucky. There are forests in the northern part of the country, while the southern area—the section that is called Herzegovina—has a great deal of farmland. This region produces wheat, corn, and sugar, as well as milk and meat.

Above: A young Muslim refugee girl wears a traditional headscarf.
Right: Damaged buildings stand in Sarajevo.

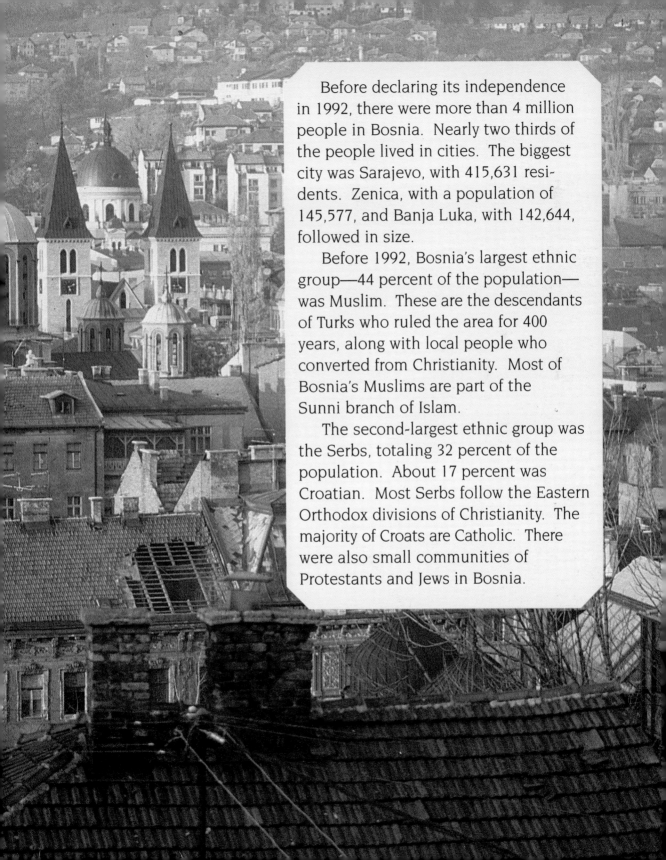

Before declaring its independence in 1992, there were more than 4 million people in Bosnia. Nearly two thirds of the people lived in cities. The biggest city was Sarajevo, with 415,631 residents. Zenica, with a population of 145,577, and Banja Luka, with 142,644, followed in size.

Before 1992, Bosnia's largest ethnic group—44 percent of the population—was Muslim. These are the descendants of Turks who ruled the area for 400 years, along with local people who converted from Christianity. Most of Bosnia's Muslims are part of the Sunni branch of Islam.

The second-largest ethnic group was the Serbs, totaling 32 percent of the population. About 17 percent was Croatian. Most Serbs follow the Eastern Orthodox divisions of Christianity. The majority of Croats are Catholic. There were also small communities of Protestants and Jews in Bosnia.

Opposite: Josip Tito headed the Yugoslavian government until his death in 1980.

The blending of different ethnic groups made bustling cities like Sarajevo fascinating places to be. The Bosnian, Serbian, and Croatian cultures seemed to blend together nicely, and there was much intermarriage between the three groups. But, below the surface, there was always tension.

In 1914, the heir to Austria-Hungary's throne, Archduke Francis Ferdinand, was murdered by a Serb in Sarajevo. This sent many European nations into what became World War I.

The war ended in 1918, leaving the whole region destroyed. That year, Bosnia became part of a new country called the Kingdom of Serbs, Croats, and Slovenes. In 1929, the nation's king, Alexander, renamed the country Yugoslavia— or "Land of the South Slavs." (Slavs was the general term for the region's peoples.)

During World War II, a Croat named Josip Broz Tito led much of the fighting against pro-Nazi forces in the country. Once the war ended in 1945, he became head of the government and ruled Yugoslavia with an iron hand. Tito, like the leaders of the Soviet Union, was a Communist. He placed severe restrictions on the press and opposition political parties. As a strong ruler, he managed to prevent Yugoslavia's various ethnic groups from fighting one another.

Opposite: Soldiers prepare to fire on the enemy during a battle on a Bosnian hillside.

On May 4, 1980, Tito died. Unemployment was high, and people were looking for someone to solve the country's problems. Soon, ethnic groups were blaming each other. By the 1990s, Yugoslavia was ready to fall apart.

On June 25, 1991, Croatia and Slovenia declared their independence from Yugoslavia. Soldiers from the Serb-led Yugoslavian army were sent to stop the republics from leaving. They lost a ten-day war to Slovenia, and a seven-month conflict to Croatia.

In April 1992—after Bosnia and Macedonia had also declared their independence—the two remaining republics, Serbia and Montenegro, agreed to unite and call themselves the Federal Republic of Yugoslavia.

Around the time Bosnia declared its independence, war broke out. Serbs, Croats, and Muslims all battled each other. In the four and a half years of horror that followed, 200,000 people—including 17,000 children—were killed. More than 2 million people lost their homes.

The term "ethnic cleansing" made headlines during the Bosnian war. The process meant that one group was driven from an area, while a rival group moved in. The new rulers said the region was "cleansed" of the old residents.

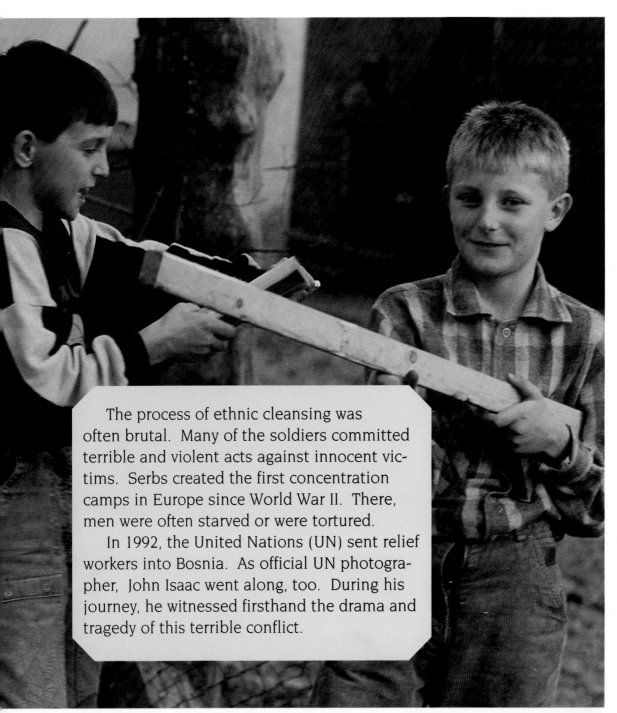

The process of ethnic cleansing was often brutal. Many of the soldiers committed terrible and violent acts against innocent victims. Serbs created the first concentration camps in Europe since World War II. There, men were often starved or were tortured.

In 1992, the United Nations (UN) sent relief workers into Bosnia. As official UN photographer, John Isaac went along, too. During his journey, he witnessed firsthand the drama and tragedy of this terrible conflict.

Two Bosnian boys play with guns they have made from scraps of wood.

It is hard to imagine that 600 years ago, the Bosnians, Serbs, and Croats were all the same. The three groups look alike and speak the same language: Serbo-Croatian. The Muslims and Croats write in the Roman alphabet—as Americans do. Serbs use the same "Cyrillic" letters as Russians. Nevertheless, everyone always understands each other in conversation.

The only thing that truly separates these three groups of people is religion. As different armies conquered the area over time, they introduced their religions to different parts of the population. Because of this one issue, individuals with so much in common have grown to hate each other.

JOHN'S STORY

I experienced hatred between ethnic groups first-hand soon after I arrived in what had been the nation of Yugoslavia. Bosnia was in flames, and many refugees had fled to a special camp in the town of Resnik, just outside the Croatian capital of Zagreb. It was there that I met an older couple whose lives had been torn apart by the war.

Above: Most of Sarajevo's historic buildings were destroyed during the war.
Below: A convoy of UNICEF trucks rolls in to help the people of Sarajevo.

"The place where we lived was attacked by Serbian people who'd grown up in Bosnia. They believed the land belonged to them," the husband said. "All the Muslims were kicked out. If my wife couldn't live there, I didn't want to live there either. But my son felt differently. He told me, 'I'm a Serb and you're a Serb. Forget about Mom. She's just a Muslim. Let her leave. Who cares what happens to her?'"

Just before the war, Bosnia's capital was one of the most magnificent cities in all of Europe. The 1984 Olympics had been held on the ski slopes just outside the city. Homes with roofs made of ceramic tiles rested on hillsides, looking down on a mix of ancient cobblestone streets and modern buildings. By 1992, Serbian fighters were in those hills. They fired shells on people of all ethnic backgrounds who refused to leave the center of town.

At one point, UNICEF—the United National International Children's Emergency Fund—arranged a "week of tranquility." During this time, the Bosnians, Croats, and Serbs all agreed to end their fighting for seven days. UNICEF brought children some of the food, medicine, and clothing they'd need for the coming winter.

 One of my most touching memories is of a visit to a school in Sarajevo. When I entered the school, the first thing I saw was the children's artwork displayed on the walls. Instead of sunny pictures of kids playing and flowers blooming, the drawings that hung there were brutal pictures of war: scared people, bombs falling on buildings, destruction and sadness. The kids sang songs about peace and proudly displayed banners of peace signs and doves.

As we were all enjoying ourselves, a loud thud stopped us dead in our tracks. A rocket had crashed into the middle of the city. The walls of the school shook, but many kids didn't react at all. The noises of war were just part of day-to-day life for them.

To the children of Bosnia, every moment was one of risk. Each day, loved ones were gunned down by shells and bullets, and kids were rushed to the hospital after wandering unknowingly into a crossfire.

This drawing, done by a young Bosnian schoolchild, shows the sadness and pain of living in the midst of war.

I'll never forget the people I photographed at Kosovo Hospital in Sarajevo. There was Azra, a dark-haired, 30-year-old woman who'd lost her husband and four-month-old baby. She'd broken her leg, but her four-year-old son escaped without injury. Now, he visited her every day. He sat beside her hospital bed and comforted her, as they waited for the war to end.

There was Sejla, a 15-year-old girl whose legs were injured in a bombing. One second, she'd been a typical teenager, walking to her friend's house. The next second, she couldn't walk at all. Fortunately, she received medical treatment and was soon on her feet again.

At an orphanage in Sarajevo, I met a group of youngsters who'd lost their parents in the city of Gorazde. At one time, 50,000 Muslims had lived there. Then, a group of Bosnian-born Serbs claimed the city as their own, and demanded that all others leave. Now, Gorazde was a bloody battlefield.

There was no heat in the orphanage, so the children kept warm by sitting around a bonfire in the courtyard. They adopted all other orphans—including cats who'd also lost their families in the fighting.

Above: An injured girl waits for care at Sarajevo's Kosovo Hospital.
Left: Youngsters at an orphanage in Sarajevo use a bonfire to stay warm.

Right: Muslim refugees living in an abandoned boxcar in Croatia.
Below: Most of the historic city of Mostar was reduced to rubble during the war.

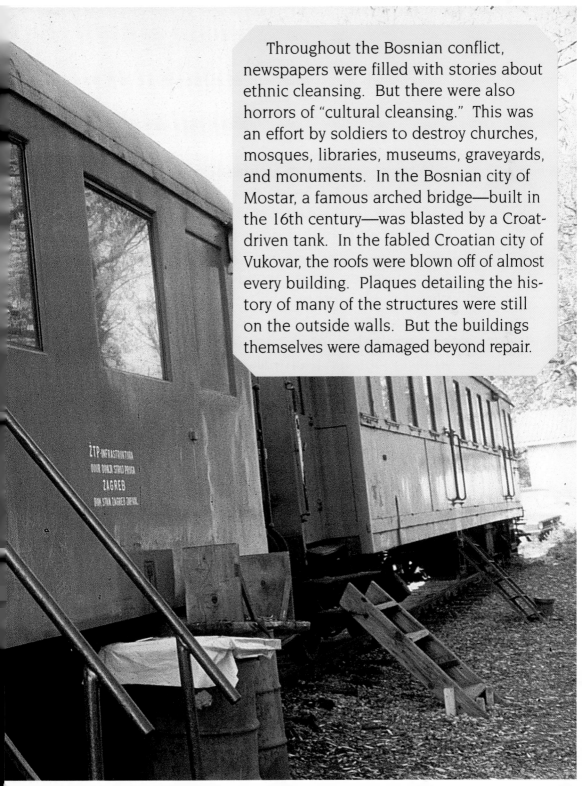

Throughout the Bosnian conflict, newspapers were filled with stories about ethnic cleansing. But there were also horrors of "cultural cleansing." This was an effort by soldiers to destroy churches, mosques, libraries, museums, graveyards, and monuments. In the Bosnian city of Mostar, a famous arched bridge—built in the 16th century—was blasted by a Croat-driven tank. In the fabled Croatian city of Vukovar, the roofs were blown off of almost every building. Plaques detailing the history of many of the structures were still on the outside walls. But the buildings themselves were damaged beyond repair.

When I was in the Bosnian town of Vitez, a Muslim pointed to a group of Gypsies and told me, "If you think we're suffering, talk to them."

The Gypsies were forced to live on the outskirts of town, and had to poke through garbage to survive. When the Muslims were in control of Vitez, they made the Gypsies do dirty jobs for them, like digging ditches. When the Serbs took over, they bossed the Gypsies around and called them names.

Yet, the Gypsies seemed to be happy. Families were close, spending their nights singing together. When UNICEF workers brought the children chocolate and school books, the young people danced for us, to the music of the accordion and other instruments. I had to admire these people who managed to find joy in the world even under the worst conditions.

At a cemetery in Zvornic, a Bosnian woman grieves the loss of a loved one

On April 28, 1995, a Croat stabbed a Serb driver to death at a gas station near the Croatian capital of Zagreb. In return, a group of Serbs closed off sections of the highway and killed three Croatian drivers.

After sitting out the war for three years, Croatia renewed its fight for territory ruled by the Serbs. With the Serbs distracted by these new battles, the Bosnians attacked. The Bosnians won back 1,500 square miles of Serb-held territory in western Bosnia.

By now, all three sides were weary and ready to talk peace. In November 1995, the presidents of the three warring countries—Serbia's Slobodan Milosevic, Croatia's Franjo Tudjman, and Bosnia's Alija Izetbegovic—accepted an American invitation to come to Dayton, Ohio, to sign a peace treaty. Under the agreement, American troops would travel to the region and help soldiers from other countries enforce the truce.

U.S. president Bill Clinton declared, "One thing I am convinced of...is that there is a global hunger among young people for their parents to put down the madness of war."

The leaders of the warring countries met to discuss peace in November 1995. U.S. secretary of state Warren Christopher helped to lead the discussions.

UN peacekeepers stand watch near Vitez, making sure that the truce is maintained.

As the agreement was being signed, I thought of an image I had seen in Sarajevo. As I was standing on a roof near the center of the city, I noticed a Muslim mosque, a Jewish synagogue, a Catholic church, and an Eastern Orthodox chapel all close to each other. Not long before, everybody there had been neighbors. Many had even been friends. With that image in my mind, I looked forward to a day in the near future when peace might allow those people to rebuild their lives and even their friendships. Perhaps then the children of the region, who had been forced to spend their young years in the midst of war, would finally have a chance to feel the many joys of childhood.

Three young Muslim boys walk hand in hand through a camp that housed more than 5,000 refugees.

FURTHER READING

Flint, David. *Bosnia: Can There Ever Be Peace?* Chatham, NJ: Raintree Steck-Vaughn, 1995.

Ricchiardi, Sherry. *Bosnia: The Struggle for Peace.* Brookfield, CT: Millbrook, 1996.

Ricciuti, Edward R. *War in Yugoslavia: Breakup of a Nation.* Brookfield, CT: Millbrook, 1994

Rody, Martyn. *The Breakup of Yugoslavia.* Morristown, NJ: Silver Burdett, 1994.

INDEX

PHOTO CREDITS

All photos ©John Isaac except: page 8: Wide World Photos; page 11: ©Laurent Van Der Stockt/Gamma-Liaison; pages 16–17: Children of Croatia/Bosnian Art Project; page 20: ©Krpan Jasmin/Gamma-Liaison; pages 26–27: ©Ralf-Finn Hestoft/Saba.